THIS **ELEPHANT & PIGGIE** BOOK
BELONGS TO:

_____

_____

_____

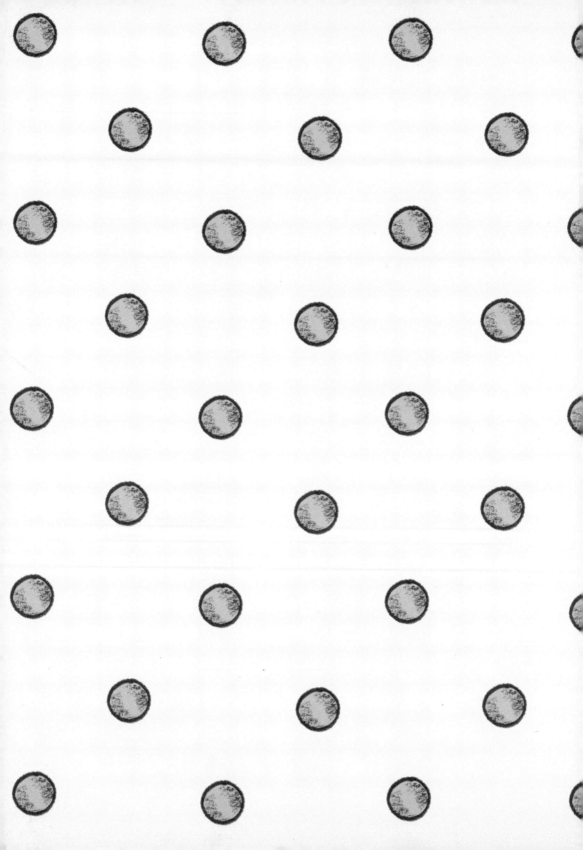

For Max, Sam, Amanda and Irving

Watch Me Throw the Ball!

By **Mo Willems**

An **ELEPHANT & PIGGIE** Book

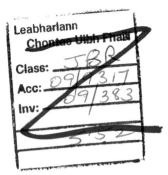
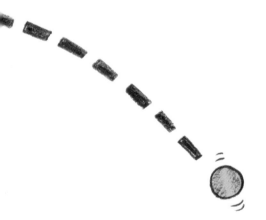

La, la, la!

You found my ball!

This is
your ball?

Yes. I threw it
from way over there!

I am very good at throwing.

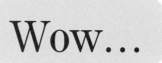

Wow...

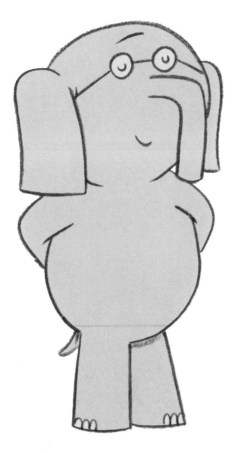

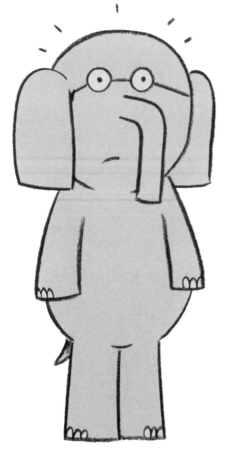

You want to
throw my ball?

Yes!

Do you know the secret
to throwing?

FUN?!

Throwing this ball is not easy!

It takes skill.
It takes practice.

It takes skill
and practice.

I worked very hard
to learn how to
throw a ball.

Very. Hard.

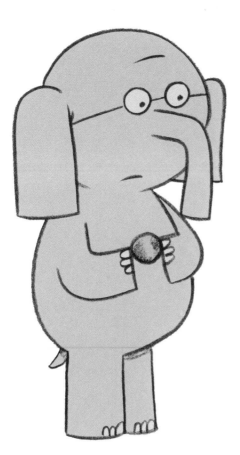

Got it.

May I
try now?

Yes.

Maybe one day you can throw like me. But—

ZIP!

THE PIG IS

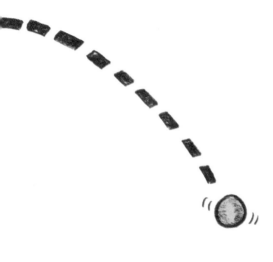

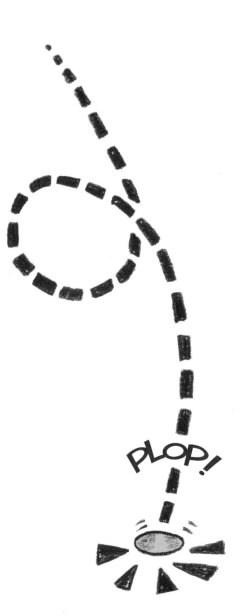

Woo!
Woooooo!

You mean "Super Pig", right?

"Super Pig", I can
see your ball …

... back here.

Do you know
what this means?

The pig does it again!!!

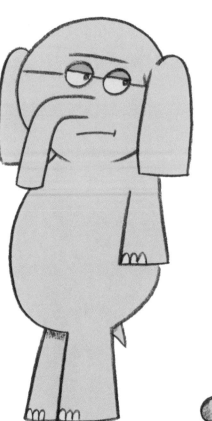

PIGGIE, YOU DID NOT THROW THE BALL AROUND THE WORLD!!!

The ball flew behind you and fell here!

And that is not very far!

Not very far at all...

You are right, Gerald. I did not really throw the ball very far.

FLING!

Woo!
Woo!

Yes!

I rock!

Mo Willems is the author of the Caldecott Honor-winning books
Knuffle Bunny: A Cautionary Tale and *Don't Let the Pigeon Drive the Bus!*
His other groundbreaking books include *Leonardo the Terrible Monster*; *Edwina, the
Dinosaur Who Didn't Know She Was Extinct* and *There Is a Bird on Your Head!*,
which won the American Library Association's 2008 Theodor Seuss Geisel Award
for the most distinguished book for beginner readers.

Mo began his career as a writer and animator on *Sesame Street*,
where he garnered six Emmy Awards.

This is a work of fiction. Names, characters, places and incidents are either
the product of the author's imagination or, if real, are used fictitiously.

First published in Great Britain 2009 by Walker Books Ltd
87 Vauxhall Walk, London SE11 5HJ

2 4 6 8 10 9 7 5 3 1

© 2009 Mo Willems

First published in the United States by Hyperion Books for Children.
British publication rights arranged with Sheldon Fogelman Agency, Inc.

The right of Mo Willems to be identified as author and illustrator of this work has been
asserted by him in accordance with the Copyright, Designs and Patents Act 1988

This book has been typeset in Century 725 and Grilled Cheese

Printed in Singapore

British Library Cataloguing in Publication Data:
a catalogue record for this book is available from the British Library

ISBN 978-1-4063-2219-4

www.walker.co.uk

www.pigeonpresents.com